Dear Parent:

Congratulations! Your child is taking the first steps on an exciting journey. The destination? Independent reading!

D0447251

STEP INTO READING® will help your child get there. The program offers books at five levels that accompany children from their first attempts at reading to reading success. Each step includes fun stories, fiction and nonfiction, and colorful art. There are also Step into Reading Sticker Books, Step into Reading Math Readers, Step into Reading Write-In Readers, Step into Reading Phonics Readers, and Step into Reading Phonics First Steps! Boxed Sets—a complete literacy program with something to interest every child.

Learning to Read, Step by Step!

Ready to Read Preschool–Kindergarten
• big type and easy words • rhyme and rhythm • picture clues
For children who know the alphabet and are eager to begin reading.

Reading with Help Preschool–Grade 1
• basic vocabulary • short sentences • simple stories
For children who recognize familiar words and sound out new words with help.

Reading on Your Own Grades 1–3
• engaging characters • easy-to-follow plots • popular topics
For children who are ready to read on their own.

Reading Paragraphs Grades 2–3
• challenging vocabulary • short paragraphs • exciting stories
For newly independent readers who read simple sentences with confidence.

Ready for Chapters Grades 2–4
• chapters • longer paragraphs • full-color art
For children who want to take the plunge into chapter books but still like colorful pictures.

STEP INTO READING® is designed to give every child a successful reading experience. The grade levels are only guides. Children can progress through the steps at their own speed, developing confidence in their reading, no matter what their grade.

Remember, a lifetime love of reading starts with a single step!

For Anna Levine, who always loved this story; for
Jennifer Arena, who always loved its folktale quality;
and for my mother, "B," who has always loved me.
—B.W.B.

Text copyright © 2005 by Beth Wagner Brust.
Illustrations copyright © 2005 by Jenny Mattheson.
All rights reserved under International and Pan-American Copyright Conventions. Published
in the United States by Random House Children's Books, a division of Random House, Inc.,
New York, and simultaneously in Canada by Random House of Canada Limited, Toronto.

www.stepintoreading.com

Educators and librarians, for a variety of teaching tools, visit us at
www.randomhouse.com/teachers

Library of Congress Cataloging-in-Publication Data
Brust, Beth Wagner.
The great tulip trade / by Beth Wagner Brust ; illustrated by Jenny Mattheson. — 1st ed.
    p.   cm. — (Step into reading. Step 3)
SUMMARY: In Holland in the 1600s, a birthday gift of eight precious tulip bulbs is traded into
livestock, furniture, and a valuable painting.
ISBN 0-375-82573-8 (pbk.) — ISBN 0-375-92573-2 (lib. bdg.)
[1. Netherlands—History—17th century—Juvenile fiction. 2. Netherlands—History—17th
century—Fiction. 3. Tulips—Fiction. 4. Barter—Fiction. 5. Birthdays—Fiction. 6. Fathers and
daughters—Fiction.] I. Mattheson, Jenny, ill. II. Title. III. Series.
PZ7.B82878Gs 2005   [Fic]—dc22   2004008067

Printed in the United States of America   First Edition   10 9 8 7 6 5 4 3 2 1

STEP INTO READING, RANDOM HOUSE, and the Random House colophon are registered trademarks
of Random House, Inc.

STEP INTO READING® STEP 3

The Great Tulip Trade

by Beth Wagner Brust

illustrated by Jenny Mattheson

Random House New York

CONCORDIA UNIVERSITY LIBRARY
PORTLAND, OR 97211

Anna loved tulips.

She loved their round shape

and bright colors

and slim green leaves.

But in Holland in 1636,
everyone loved tulips!
That made tulips worth
more than gold and diamonds.
More than almost anything.

One spring morning,

Anna saw her father cutting tulips.

People wanted the bulbs the most.

"Stop, Papa!" said Anna.

"Sorry, Birthday Girl," he said.
"My bulbs in the ground
  grow bigger and better
  without the flower."
"Please, let me have some tulips
  for my birthday," begged Anna.

"Very well," he said.
"You may choose eight
since you are now eight."
"Thank you!" said Anna.

First, she chose two red ones.

Then two yellow ones.

A purple one.

A pink-and-white-striped one.

A red one with yellow edges
that looked like flames.

Then her favorite tulip.

The rarest tulip of all,

the Semper Augustus.

Anna put all the tulips

in her wheelbarrow

and pushed it to their cottage.

She planted them in a window box.

Soon she saw a farmer
bringing his sheep and cows
to market.

"What pretty tulips!" he said.

"I'll trade you for a red tulip.

And a yellow one," he said.

The farmer thought

he could sell the tulips

for more than his sheep and cows.

"Sorry, they're not for sale,"

said Anna.

"They are my birthday present."

"I'll give you a lamb,"

said the farmer.

"No, thank you," said Anna.

He held up another lamb.

"I'll give you two lambs,

a cow, and a puppy."

Anna felt bad.

The tulips were her present.

But with lambs,

her family could spin the wool

to make into cloth.

With a cow, they could have
fresh milk, butter, and cheese.
And the puppy would grow bigger
and protect their tulip field.

Besides, Anna would still
have six tulips left.
"All right, I'll trade," she said.

A while later, a peddler and
his wife stopped their wagon.
"What lovely flowers!"
called the peddler.
"I'll trade you some pots and pans
for the pink-striped one."

The peddler knew
that he could sell
the tulip for more than
his pots and pans.
"No, thank you," said Anna.

"Add the red one,"

said the man,

"and you may have

this warm wool rug."

Anna looked at the rug.

She looked at her red tulip.

Their stone floor was cold.

A rug would be nice.

Four tulips would be left.

She would still have her favorite,

the very rare Semper Augustus.

"All right," she said.

Anna took the rug

and pots and pans.

At noon, an artist walked by.

"What a picture-perfect tulip!"

he said.

"Thank you," said Anna.

"Would you trade that purple tulip
for a painting?" he asked.
He knew it would be worth
more than twenty paintings.

"No, thank you," said Anna.
"They are my birthday present."

"Painted flowers never wilt,"

said the artist.

He turned his board around.

Anna gasped.

She had never seen

such a pretty picture!

Anna thought about
the bare cottage walls.
"I will trade," she said.
The artist gave Anna the painting.
"Happy birthday," he said.

Soon a wagon heaped
with furniture pulled up.
"I must buy that flamed tulip!"
called the furniture maker.
"It is not for sale," said Anna.

"I'll trade you this cabinet for it,"
the man said.

"No," said Anna.

"The cabinet, a dining table,
and six chairs?" he asked.

Anna knew they could use a cabinet.

And they needed a bigger table.

But NO!

These three tulips were her last!

"Sorry," said Anna. "No trade."

The man's face turned
as red as the tulip.
"Impossible!" he cried.
"Give me the yellow one, too,
and I'll give you all that *and*
a bed with a feather mattress."

A real bed!

Now *that* was special!

Her family would sleep on a bed

instead of on hard boards.

"Yes," said Anna.

"Here comes Papa!"

shouted Anna's brother.

Anna looked at her window box.

Oh, dear! Only one tulip was left.

What would Papa say?

Suddenly, a coach pulled up.

"Ooooooohh!" squealed a woman.

"I *must* have that tulip!"

The mayor leaned out the window.

"Girl, how much for that flower?"

"It's not for sale," said Anna.

"Nonsense!" he said.

"My lady wants that flower."

Anna looked at her father.

"Where are your other tulips?"

asked Papa.

Anna's brother spoke first.

"Anna traded them for a table,

pots and pans,

a painting and a puppy,

a bed and a rug,

a cabinet and a cow,

two lambs, and six chairs!"

Papa stepped back.

"For seven tulips,

you got all that?" he said.

Anna nodded.

"But this is my favorite.

I'm keeping it for my birthday."

"I'll trade this gold necklace

for it," the mayor shouted.

Anna shook her head.

"*And* this diamond bracelet

and these gold coins!"

Anna shook her head.

The mayor looked ready to explode.
"The jewelry, the money,

and a big house!" he shouted.

"All for one tulip."

Anna's father took her aside.

"Am I stupid not to want to trade?"

asked Anna.

"No," said her father.
"It is your choice.
But today, your rare tulip
is worth a big house.
Tomorrow, no one may want tulips.
They may be worth nothing at all."

Anna nodded.

She thought she understood.

"Well?" called the mayor.

"Is it mine?" asked his wife.

Anna put the Semper Augustus
in a clay pot.

The mayor reached out.

Anna didn't move.

"I will not trade

my very last birthday tulip.

It is a gift from my father.

That makes it worth more to me

than anything else."

Author's Note

In Holland in the 1600s, people loved tulips. Some people bought tulip bulbs with Dutch money called florins. Others traded their animals, jewelry, gold, and land for tulips. This made the price keep going up. A tulip bulb cost a hundred florins one day. The next day, it was worth much more. People saw buying and selling tulip bulbs as a way to get rich.

The Semper Augustus really was the most rare and expensive tulip. One sold for 4,600 florins, a coach, and a pair of horses.

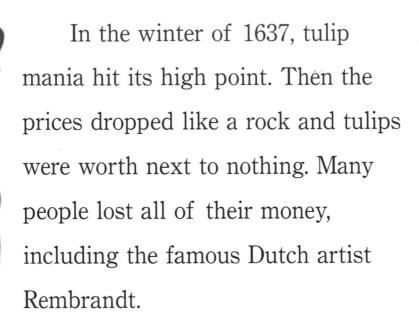

In the winter of 1637, tulip mania hit its high point. Then the prices dropped like a rock and tulips were worth next to nothing. Many people lost all of their money, including the famous Dutch artist Rembrandt.

All this for an ugly little bulb that looked like an onion but turned into the loveliest of flowers!

C.Lit PZ 7 .B82878 Gs 2005
Brust, Beth Wagner.
The great tulip trade